Licensed exclusively to Top That Publishing Ltd
Tide Mill Way, Woodbridge, Suffolk, IP12 1AP, UK
www.topthatpublishing.com
Copyright © 2018 Tide Mill Media
All rights reserved
2 4 6 8 9 7 5 3
Manufactured in China

Illustrated by Daniel Howarth
Written by Peter Shaw

ISBN 978-1-84956-778-7

A catalogue record for this book is available from the British Library

Little Ronnie and Magic the Horse

Written by Peter Shaw

'For Jessica, my inspiration,
My little ray of sunshine,
You'll never know a love as strong,
As the love you'll get of mine.

From your loving Daddy x'
Peter Shaw

Ronnie was delighted with his new birthday toy,
A white rocking horse that was just right for a boy.
With a long purple tail and a silky mane,
Ronnie decided to give it a name.

'You'll be "Magic" ... "Magic the horse".'
Ronnie never thought Magic would be magic, of course!
He jumped on the stallion, without looking back.
The room started swirling, before it turned black ...

Now Magic was real, and they no longer stood,
In Ronnie's bedroom, but a mysterious wood.

There were flowers and trees, but where was his bed?
And in place of a wardrobe there were rocks instead!

Beyond the trees was a castle in the distance,
Ronnie could scarcely believe its existence.
So off they sped, to meet the Queen and King,
Of the enchanted world they found themselves in.

Soon they arrived and they were met at the gates,
By a guard who was grumpy and a bit overweight.
'You're late,' he said. 'You'd better go in.
You're braver than me, being late for the King!'

They followed his directions to the King's quarters,
And the hustle and bustle of the servants and porters.
'We thought you'd forgotten – at last, you've arrived!'
Cried the beautiful Queen, with tears in her eyes.

'I'm afraid there's a dragon,' the King then sighed.
'His roar can be heard from far and wide.
He's frightening our people and we've had enough.
We need your help, Ronnie,' he said, with a huff.

'I'll see what I can do, but it won't be easy,'
Said Ronnie, sounding brave, but feeling queasy.
'So giddiup, Magic,' and they galloped off with a neigh.
Would Ronnie and his noble steed find their way?

A few hours passed (and gosh they went fast),
When a roar filled the air – they'd found
the dragon at last ...

'Is that him, Magic?' asked Ronnie, with a snigger.
'He doesn't look scary and I thought he'd be bigger!'
He was slimy and scaly, but most strangely of all,
The troublesome dragon was incredibly small!

'We can't fight this dragon; he's done nothing wrong.
We'll go back to the castle, and take him along.
We can't leave him here all on his own,
Perhaps he'll stop roaring if we give him a home.'

So back to the castle and to the King's quarters,
And the hustle and bustle of the servants and porters.
'Allow me to introduce ...' Ronnie said, with a smile,
'The dragon that's caused trouble all this while.'

'Is it true,' laughed the Queen, 'that this little thing,
Has scared all the people and even the King?'

'It's true,' said Ronnie, 'and I've got an idea!
It will stop him from roaring throughout the year.
Why not give him a home, his very own house?
And in return he will be as quiet as a mouse.'

They agreed to the deal, and the dragon was invited,
To live by the castle; he was truly delighted!

Ronnie turned up that evening for his reward,
Riding on Magic, he was greeted with applause.
Ronnie was happy; he felt extremely excited,
As he knelt before the King, ready to be knighted.

'Arise, Sir Ronnie,' and the crowd cheered.
Ronnie looked up … but they'd all disappeared!

Now Ronnie was back in his bedroom once more,
There was his bed and his old chest of drawers.
'I got off Magic,' Ronnie said with dismay,
'And it made my adventure vanish away.'

And sure enough, Magic stood wooden and lifeless,
But Ronnie knew Magic WAS magic and priceless.